Barbie™
The Pearl Princess

A Panorama Sticker Storybook

Based on the screenplay by Cydne Clark & Steve Granat
Illustrated by Ulkutay Design Group

Special thanks to Dianne Reichenberger, Cindy Ledermann, Jocelyn Morgan, Tanya Mann, Julia Phelps, Sharon Woloszyk, Rita Lichtwardt, Carla Alford, Renee Reeser Zelnick, Rob Hudnut, David Wiebe, Shelley Dvi-Vardhana, Sarah Lazar, Gabrielle Miles, Rainmaker Entertainment, and Walter P. Martishius.

Reader's Digest
Children's Books®

New York, New York • Montréal, Québec • Bath, United Kingdom

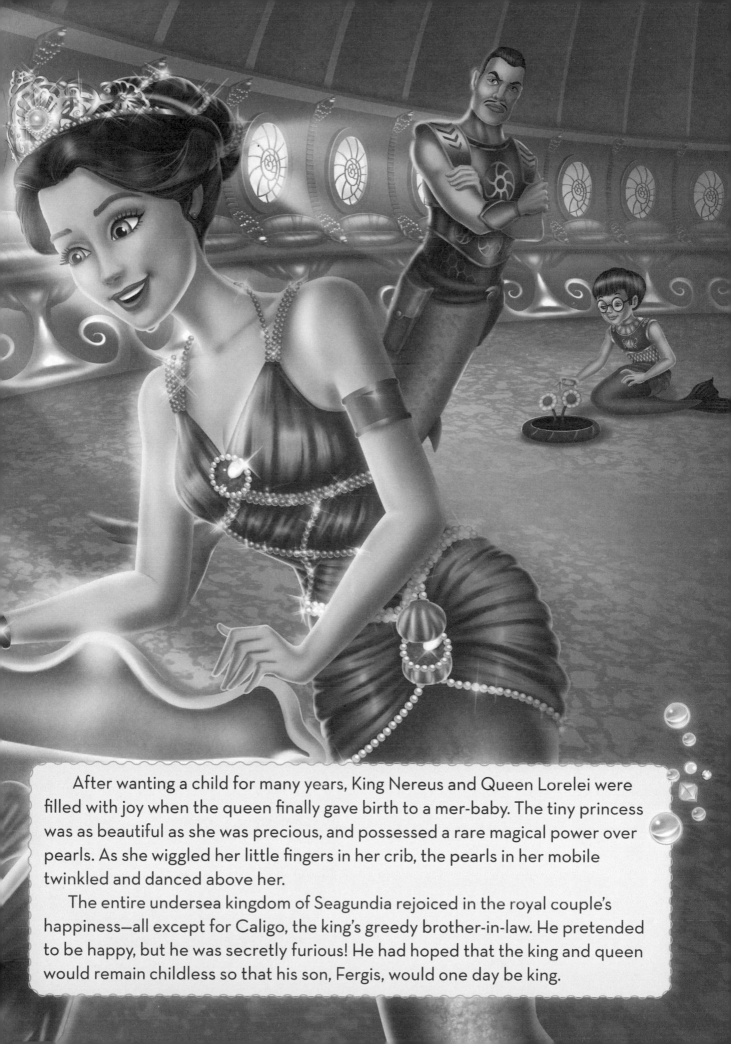

After wanting a child for many years, King Nereus and Queen Lorelei were filled with joy when the queen finally gave birth to a mer-baby. The tiny princess was as beautiful as she was precious, and possessed a rare magical power over pearls. As she wiggled her little fingers in her crib, the pearls in her mobile twinkled and danced above her.

The entire undersea kingdom of Seagundia rejoiced in the royal couple's happiness—all except for Caligo, the king's greedy brother-in-law. He pretended to be happy, but he was secretly furious! He had hoped that the king and queen would remain childless so that his son, Fergis, would one day be king.

Caligo had always wanted to rule the kingdom, and still planned to do so once Fergis inherited the throne. To ensure that his plan stayed intact, he paid a poor sorceress named Scylla to get rid of the princess.

As Scylla secretly lifted the baby out of her crib, something magical happened—the princess's smile melted the woman's cold heart! Scylla instantly fell in love with the child. *I need to keep the girl safe from Caligo,* she thought. Therefore, instead of doing away with the child, she tenderly wrapped the baby in a blanket and fled to a hidden reef in the farthest corner of the sea.

Scylla named the baby Lumina, and raised her and loved her. She
made the reef into a bright and cheery home where she hoped that no
one—especially Caligo—would ever find them. Lumina loved playing
with her pearl magic, but Scylla always insisted that she use it privately—
she didn't want anyone to become suspicious that she was royalty.

Lumina grew up happy, never knowing that she was a princess, but
like all little girls, she always dreamed of what it was like to be one.

As a beautiful young mer-woman, Lumina liked to pretend to be a princess with her best friend Kuda, a pink seahorse. "I wonder what a real princess looks like," she said, as they pretended to perform a royal coronation.

Lumina reached into her pouch and tossed out a handful of pearls. The pearls danced and twinkled all around them as they lined up to float grandly in the procession.

Through the cave's wall, Scylla listened to the girls talk about castles and princesses. She had always felt guilty about taking the child from the king and queen. She opened the shell-covered box that safely kept the princess's baby bracelet and decided to finally tell the girl the truth about her royal identity.

"Lumina," she called, "there's something I need to tell you."

"What is it, Aunt Scylla?" Lumina replied as she was styling Kuda's new princess-do with pearls.

"Oh...nothing," Scylla stammered, suddenly thinking the better of it.

Meanwhile, across the sea, Caligo was scheming his way to the throne. "We suppose you are right," said the mournful king and queen. "After seventeen years, it is time to confirm upon the heir apparent our royal emblem—the Pearl of the Sea."

"Excellent!" Caligo grinned. "We'll throw a royal ball for Fergis to choose a suitable wife, too," he said glancing at his mer-nerd son who was admiring his plant collection.

To execute his plan, Caligo sent his eel, Murray, to find Scylla. This time, he wanted Scylla to give the king a potion that would make him unfit to rule the kingdom. Then, Fergis would become king that night!

"I'm not in that business anymore," Scylla replied angrily to Murray who had found her hidden home and told her of Caligo's request.

"Caligo thought you would say that," said Murray, as he handed her an invitation to the ball. "If you don't do it, he will tell everyone that you did away with the princess."

Scylla was gathering her things for the long trip to the castle when Lumina begged her to let her come along.

"The journey is far too dangerous," explained Scylla. "I only go to sell my potions."

Disappointed, Lumina said good-bye. Moments later, she found the invitation to the ball on the table.

"She can't get in without this," Lumina exclaimed to Kuda. "So it is our duty to bring it to her—even if we have to go all the way to the castle!" she explained, justifying her disobedience to Scylla's request to stay home.

The girls were making their way through the dangerous ocean when suddenly, a stonefish frightened them.

Lumina quickly waved her hands and a large pearl landed on each poisonous spike of the deadly creature, taking away its ferocious power.

"Why did you do that?" asked Spike the stonefish angrily. "No one will ever be afraid of me now."

"Just be nice," said Lumina. "Come to the royal city with us. You can practice being friendly there," she offered.

"You don't mind?" asked Spike, unfamiliar with such kindness.

"I'd be honored," said Lumina, as Kuda uneasily agreed.

As the friends continued their journey through the ocean, Spike helped them navigate their way through burning coral and vampire squid. Soon they came to a cliff overlooking Mermaid City. "The castle!" they cried.

"It's even more beautiful than I imagined," exclaimed Lumina. "I can't believe we're here!"

As the girls admired the splendor of the city, Spike practiced being friendly. The mermaids liked him!

"Hey, there's Scylla!" Kuda pointed out as she saw Scylla swim out of a shop. "Do you have the invitation?"

"Oh, no! I must have lost it in all that kelp," Lumina said,
panicked that Scylla would be furious that they made the journey
against her wishes. The girls raced into a nearby hair salon to hide.
Lumina began styling a client's hair with Kuda as her assistant.

"It's gorgeous!" a boisterous voice shouted waving her
tentacles. "You've got the job!"

It was Madame Ruckus, the owner of the busy beauty salon. She needed another hair stylist to help all the mermaids get ready for the royal ball—Lumina was the perfect choice.

Thrilled, Lumina used her pearl magic to create trendy new styles that all the mermaids wanted. Madame Ruckus even gave Lumina and Kuda an invitation to attend the royal ball that night!

At the castle, Murray reported to Caligo that the princess was alive. The royal crest on the baby bracelet that Murray took from Scylla's cave confirmed his suspicion that Lumina was indeed the princess. Caligo seethed. "This ruins everything! Find her and get rid of her!" he demanded.

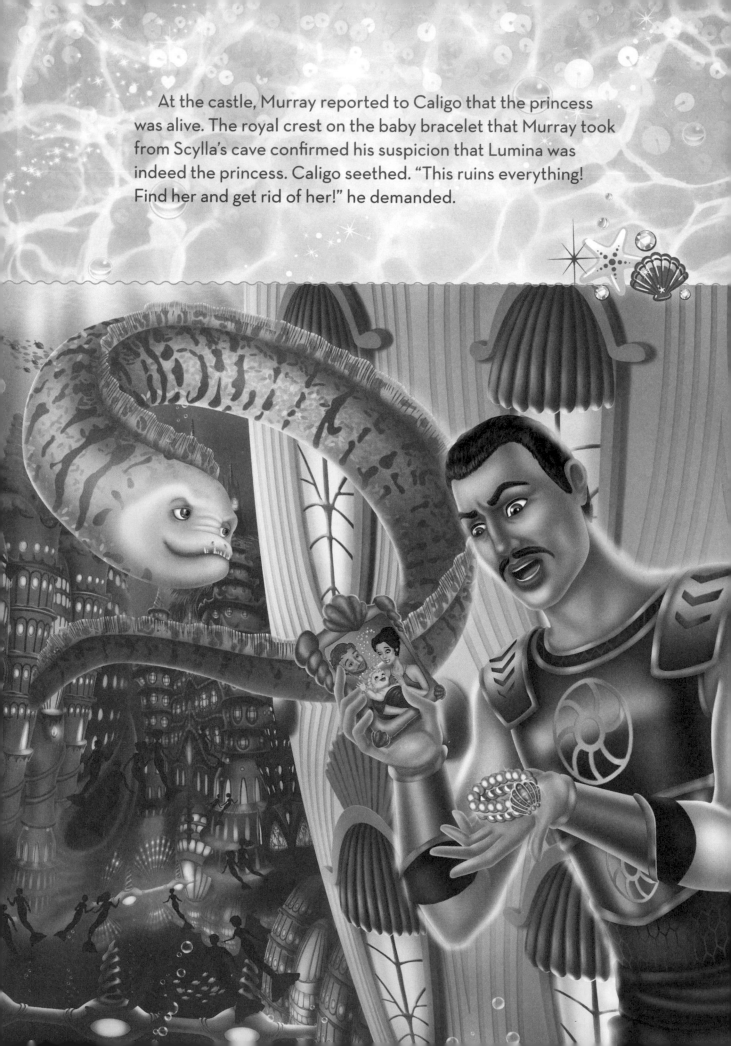

As the ball began, Caligo checked on Scylla in the castle's beverage closet. She was readying her potions. "You will give the king the tainted cup when you serve the royal party their drinks," he ordered her.

Lumina and Kuda were thrilled to be in a real castle at a real royal ball. They had so much fun getting dressed up for the occasion, and were having a spectacular time dancing in the ballroom when Murray suddenly captured the girls and brought them to the castle's dungeon. He locked them up and told them that Scylla was going to harm the king.

"Scylla wouldn't do that," Lumina told Murray. Then, when he wasn't looking, she took off her pearl necklace and used her magic to make the strands loop around the key ring and carry it back to her. She opened the lock with the key.

The girls rushed into the ballroom where they saw Scylla serving the king his drink. Afraid that Murray was right, Lumina lunged toward the king and knocked the cup out of his hands.

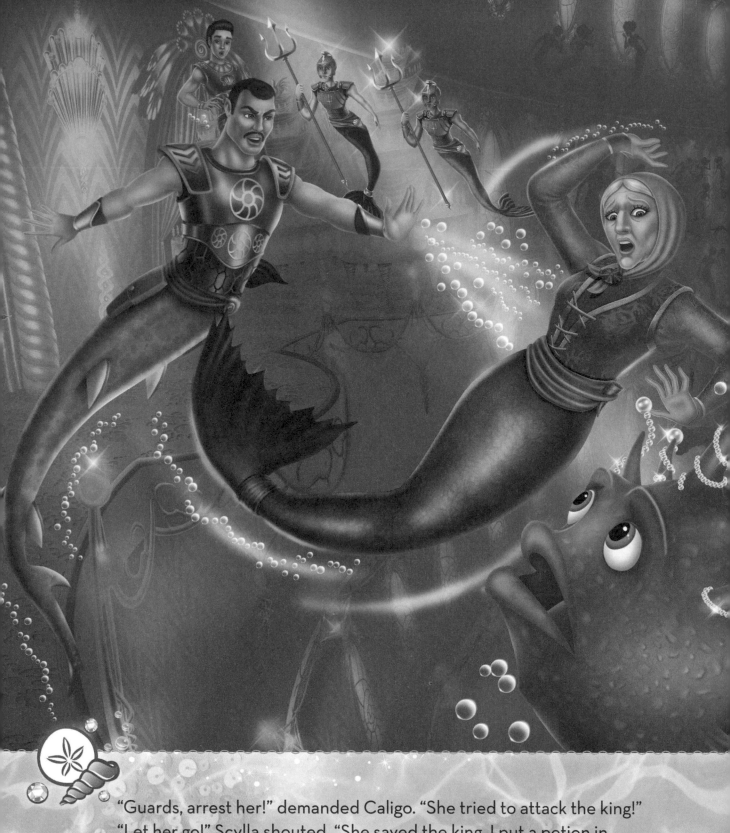

"Guards, arrest her!" demanded Caligo. "She tried to attack the king!"

"Let her go!" Scylla shouted. "She saved the king. I put a potion in his cup!"

Suddenly nervous that Scylla was going to reveal the truth about his evil plan, Caligo plucked a pearl off one of Spike's poisonous spears and shoved her into it.

"Aunt Scylla!" Lumina shouted as she ran over to her.

As she gasped for breath, Scylla finally told Lumina the truth about her identity.

"Long ago I took you from the king and queen. I did it to protect you from Caligo, but I should have returned you a long time ago. I just didn't want to lose you."

Wanting to help Scylla, Fergis handed Lumina a sulfur lily. "Put the petals on her tongue," he said. "It's the only remedy to cure her."

As Scylla regained her strength, she told the king that Caligo was the one who wanted her to give him the harmful potion, and that he ordered her to get rid of the princess seventeen years ago, too.

Suddenly, at the king's request, the palace guards rushed in and took Caligo away.

"Welcome home," the king and queen said to Lumina, overcome with emotion.

"Home? Here in the castle?" Lumina asked, surprised. Scylla reassured her with a nod.

Lumina wrapped her arms around the king and queen. "You are my parents?" she asked, still trying to make sense of it all.

"Yes," they said smiling. "And it wouldn't be home for you unless Scylla and Kuda lived here, too."

The music resumed as Fergis removed the Pearl of the Sea emblem from his uniform and handed it to Lumina. "This is rightfully yours," he said.

As the princess and her friends settled into the castle, life came back to the kingdom. Princess Lumina had made it a better place for everyone.